THE OLYMPIANS

LEONARD EVERETT FISHER

THE OLYMPIANS

Great Gods and Goddesses of Ancient Greece

Holiday House / New York

Bibliography

Barthell, Edward E., Jr. *Gods and Goddesses of Ancient Greece*. Miami: University of Miami Press, 1971.

Bulfinch, Thomas. *The Age of Fable*. New York: The New American Library, 1962.

Graves, Robert. *The Greek Myths*, Vols. I, II. New York: George Braziller, 1959.

Hamilton, Edith. *Mythology*. Boston: Little, Brown & Co., 1940.

Homer. *Iliad*. Translated by Richmond Lattimore. Chicago: The University of Chicago Press, 1961.

Hope, Thomas. *Costumes of the Ancients*, Vols. I, II. London: William Miller, 1812.

Loprochon, Pierre. *The Many Faces of Greece*. New York-Paris: Leon Amiel, 1975.

Virgil. *Aeneid*. Translated by Allan Mandelbaum, New York: Bantam Books, Inc., 1981.

Copyright © 1984 by Leonard Everett Fisher
All rights reserved
Printed in the United States of America
First Edition

Library of Congress Cataloging in Publication Data

Fisher, Leonard Everett.
The Olympians.

Bibliography: p.
Summary: Offers brief biographical sketches of the twelve gods and goddesses that reside on Mount Olympus including such information as their Roman names, their parents, and the symbols that represent them.
1. Gods, Greek—Juvenile literature. 2. Mythology, Greek—Juvenile literature. [1. Mythology, Greek]
I. Title.
BL782.F58   1984   292′.211   84-516
ISBN 0-8234-0522-2

THE GODS AND GODDESSES ON MOUNT OLYMPUS

Greek Name		Roman Name
Zeus ✓	King of the Gods	Jupiter
Poseidon ✓	God of the Seas	Neptune
Hades ✓	God of the Lower World	Pluto
	God of Wealth	
Hera	Queen of the Gods	Juno
Hestia	Goddess of the Hearth	Vesta
Ares	God of War	Mars
Athena	Goddess of Wisdom	Minerva
	Goddess of War	
	Goddess of Arts and Crafts	
	Goddess of the City	
Apollo ✓	God of Light and Truth	Apollo
	God of Healing	
	God of Archery	
	God of Music	
Aphrodite	Goddess of Love	Venus
	Goddess of Beauty	
Hermes ✓	God of Motion	Mercury
	God of Sleep and Dreams	
	God of Commerce	
	God of Travelers	
Artemis	Goddess of the Hunt	Diana
	Goddess of the Moon	
	Goddess of Children	
Hephaestus	God of the Forge	Vulcan

To many ancient Greeks, Mount Olympus was the home of their twelve great gods and goddesses, the "Olympians." It was and still is a high mountain in Greece. Some ancient Greeks thought of Mount Olympus as more than a real mountain. They imagined it was a place that could not be found on Earth. No matter what or where Mount Olympus was—or was not—it was thought to be peaceful and flooded with sunshine.

As for the Olympians, they looked like human beings. But they had powers unlike those of human beings. They could change themselves into creatures like eagles and bulls. They married each other. They lived forever, sipping nectar, their life-giving drink, and dining on ambrosia, their special food.

While the Olympians were the first to live on Mount Olympus, they were not the first to rule the universe and its three regions: the Skies, the Seas, and the Lower World. These they won from the Titans, a race of giants, in a mighty battle. The Titans were ruled by their father, Cronus, who had seized the powers of the universe from his own parents, Uranus and Gaea—Heaven and Earth.

Finally, when ancient Greece was conquered by the armies of Rome in 146 B.C., Greek ideas about Mount Olympus lived on. The less imaginative Romans gave the Greek gods and goddesses Roman names and worshiped them as their own.

ZEUS

King of Gods

Zeus was the most powerful god on Mount Olympus. He made the sun and moon come and go. He changed the seasons. He carried a bright shield marked with an eagle. He could cause a storm with one shake of his shield. When Zeus was angry, he hurled thunderbolts. He was the ruler of the skies. He laughed easily. And he fell in love often. Zeus's wife and queen, Hera, was always very jealous. Zeus was the chief judge of Mount Olympus and settled all disputes fairly.

Roman Name: Jupiter
Parents: Cronus and Rhea
Symbols: Eagle, Shield, Thunderbolt, Oak Tree

POSEIDON

God of the Seas

Poseidon was the second most powerful god on Mount Olympus. He won the realm of the seas after the Titans were defeated. Although married to Amphitrite, the granddaughter of a Titan, he fell in love with other women almost as often as Zeus. Poseidon spent his time between Mount Olympus and his palace beneath the sea. Always restless, he plotted to seize the lands, cities and countries of humans. He dried up the lakes and rivers of people he did not trust. And he sent great tidal waves against those who made him angry. But when he rode over the seas in his golden chariot, the waters became calm. Never still, he invented the horse and gave it to man.

Roman Name: Neptune
Parents: Cronus and Rhea
Symbols: Trident, Horse, Bull

HADES

God of the Lower World
God of Wealth

Cronus's third son, Hades, ruled over the world of the dead—the Lower World. It was a gloomy realm of wailing ghosts, howling furies, shrieking bats, lost and evil souls. Hades rarely visited Mount Olympus or the land of the living. But when he did, no one saw him. He wore a magic helmet that made him invisible. And no one who entered the Lower World was ever allowed to leave. The one exception was Persephone, Hades' wife, who lived on Earth before she became his queen. Hades owned everything precious that lay in the ground—every piece of gold and silver, every diamond, ruby, emerald and gem.

Roman Name: Pluto
Parents: Cronus and Rhea
Symbols: Helmet, Metals, Jewels

HERA

Queen of the Gods

For beautiful Hera, Zeus's wife, life on Mount Olympus was difficult. Although Zeus sought Hera's advice and help in ruling the other Olympians, Hera had little luck in managing him. She spent much of her time in jealous rages, plotting either to destroy Zeus or to punish his lady friends. Often seen with her pet peacock, Hera was adored by married women everywhere. She was worshiped by women as the protector of marriage.

Roman Name:	Juno
Parents:	Cronus and Rhea
Symbols:	Peacock, Cow

HESTIA

Goddess of the Hearth

Hestia was the sweetest, gentlest and most generous of all the Olympians. She never disagreed with anyone, and she never took sides in an argument. She was the goddess who protected the home and family although she herself never married. Every human prayed to her. And every fire in every hearth was Hestia's fire. When the home fire dimmed, the coals were kept alive and glowing to honor her. Usually, ancient Greeks carried live coals from an old city to a newly built city in her name.

Roman Name: Vesta
Parents: Cronus and Rhea
Symbol: Fire

ARES

God of War

Ares was a fiery, bloody character. Not even his parents liked him. He thrived on violence, battles and wars. The Earth growled and groaned beneath him as he moved. Even though he joined wars on Earth among humans, he was not as powerful as he appeared. There were times when he was driven from battlefields by humans who preferred living in peace to fighting one another.

Roman Name: Mars
Parents: Zeus and Hera
Symbols: Vulture, Dog

ATHENA

Goddess of Wisdom
Goddess of War
Goddess of Arts and Crafts
Goddess of the City

Athena was born fully grown from the head of Zeus, dressed in armor. She hated war, and she waged it only to defend the side of right. Athena never lost a battle. She carried a magic shield that turned her enemies to stone. The city of Athens was named after her. And in Athens, she created the olive tree. Athena invented the ship, plow, trumpet, and bridle. She knew the secrets of mathematics and taught cooking, sewing and weaving to women everywhere. Athena never married. She was Zeus's favorite child.

Roman Name: Minerva
Parents: Zeus
Symbols: Owl, Shield, Olive Branch

APOLLO

God of Light and Truth
God of Healing
God of Archery
God of Music

Apollo was perhaps the most loved of all the gods on Mount Olympus. He was handsome, talented, charming and honest. He delighted all the Olympians when he plucked his golden lyre and sang songs. He taught people how to comfort and cure the sick and ailing. He shot arrows into every monster that threatened anyone he loved. He was full of goodwill wherever he went. Many believed that Apollo spoke to humans through the voice of Pythia, a priestess called the "Delphic Oracle."

Roman Name: Apollo
Parents: Zeus and Leto
Symbols: Crow, Dolphin, Laurel, Lyre

APHRODITE

Goddess of Love
Goddess of Beauty

Some say that Aphrodite was the daughter of Zeus and
Dione. Others insist that she had no mother at all—not
even a father! Instead, she came from the foamy sea and
later appeared on Mount Olympus. There, Zeus adopted
her and gave her in marriage to Hephaestus, God of the
Forge. But Hephaestus did not interest her. Aphrodite put
on a magic belt that made other men fall in love with her.
Every goddess tried to beg, borrow or steal that belt, but
none succeeded. Aphrodite's power to love was so great
that even wild lions and tigers were tamed in her
presence.

Roman Name: Venus
Parents: Zeus and Dione
Symbols: Dove, Sparrow, Swan, Myrtle

HERMES

God of Motion
God of Sleep and Dreams
God of Commerce
God of Travelers

Hermes was graceful, clever and quick. He was Zeus's messenger. He wore a winged golden helmet—sometimes a silver one—to protect himself from bad weather. His golden winged sandles gave him speed. And he carried a magic golden wand or *caduceus,* a gift from Apollo, to guide him on his journeys. One of his jobs was to lead the dead to Hades' Lower World. Another was to watch over tradesmen and travelers. He also helped travelers sleep well and have pleasant dreams. Hermes invented fire, written music, boxing and the lyre, his gift to Apollo.

Roman Name: Mercury
Parents: Zeus and Maia
Symbols: Wand, Winged sandals, Winged helmet

ARTEMIS

Goddess of the Hunt
Goddess of the Moon
Goddess of Children

Artemis was the twin sister of Apollo. Armed with a silver bow and arrows, she chased stags and other wild animals. Yet, as Goddess of the Hunt, she protected young animals and looked after young children. In some ways Artemis acted like her brother. She could bring deadly diseases to whole cities and cure them, too. Like Apollo, who was linked to the sun as God of Light and Truth, Artemis was connected to the moon as a symbol of purity. And like Athena and Hestia, Artemis never married.

Roman Name: Diana
Parents: Zeus and Leto
Symbols: Stag, Moon, Cypress

HEPHAESTUS

God of the Forge

Of all the gods and goddesses on Mount Olympus, Hephaestus was the least good looking. In fact, his own mother hated him for his lack of looks. Also, Hephaestus was the only Olympian who was born with a handicap. He had a deformed foot. Hephaestus made armor and weapons for the gods and goddesses. He made jewelry, too. His forge was under any erupting volcano. He was unhappily married to Aphrodite, whom he worshiped but who betrayed him with a string of lovers. Hephaestus was a hard worker who was happiest at his forge. He was also gentle and good-natured.

Roman Name: Vulcan
Parents: Zeus and Hera
Symbols: Fire, Blacksmith's hammer

LEF

Family Tree

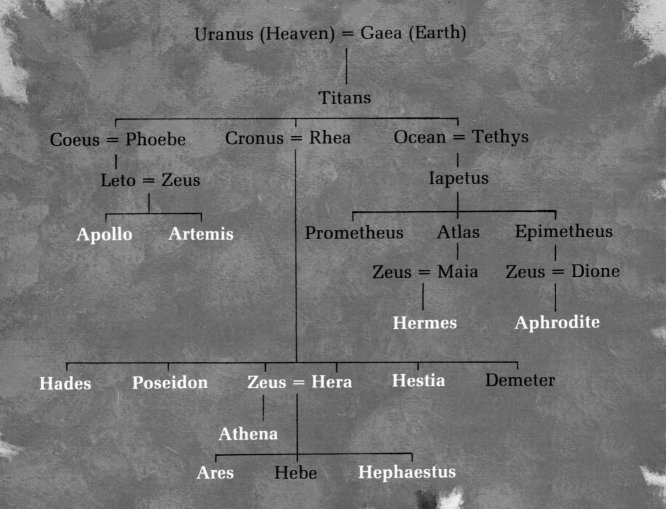

Uranus (Heaven) = Gaea (Earth)
|
Titans

Coeus = Phoebe Cronus = Rhea Ocean = Tethys

Leto = Zeus

Apollo **Artemis**

Iapetus

Prometheus Atlas Epimetheus

Zeus = Maia Zeus = Dione

Hermes **Aphrodite**

Hades **Poseidon** Zeus = Hera **Hestia** Demeter

Athena

Ares Hebe **Hephaestus**

This family tree shows Heaven an
Earth, the Titans, and four generation
of Greek gods and goddesses—si
generations in all—of the same famil
The names seen in white are the twelv
gods and goddesses in this book. Mos
scholars agree that these twelve are th
most important gods and goddesses wh
lived on Mount Olympus.

292.21   Fisher, Leonard
Fis   Everett
            Olympians

DATE DUE

C20343